CAPTAIN CAT

Property of

SELF School

An I Can Read Book®

CAPTAIN CAT

Story and pictures by
SYD HOFF

SCHOLASTIC INC.

New York Toronto London Auckland Sydney
Mexico City New Delhi Hong Kong Buenos Aires

ISBN 0-439-60808-2

12 11 10 9 8 7 6 5 4 3 2 1   4 5 6 7 8 9/0

Printed in the U.S.A.   23

First Scholastic printing, January 2004

For Nina

Captain Cat joined the army.

He went in when nobody was looking.

7

The soldiers marched in a parade.

"Left, right—

left, right . . ."

Captain Cat kept in step.

He knew one foot from the other.

"That cat has more stripes

than we have,"

said a corporal to a sergeant.

"Meow," said Captain Cat.

Another sergeant looked at the cat.

"Yes sir!" he said and laughed.

13

From then on

everybody started saying,

"Here, Captain Cat,"

when they wanted him,

instead of

"Here, kitty kitty."

But sometimes the soldiers

had no time for Captain Cat.

"I have to clean the bathrooms,"
said one soldier.

"I have to sweep the grounds,"

said another soldier.

One soldier named Pete

always found time for Captain Cat,

even when he was on guard duty.

"You remind me of a cat back home,"

he said, and scratched Captain Cat

behind the ears.

Pete played with Captain Cat so much,

he got into trouble.

The general made Pete

do kitchen duty.

Captain Cat kept him company.

Pete let Captain Cat play

with the potato peels.

"Are you my buddy?"

asked Pete.

"Me-ow," said Captain Cat.

The next morning

a bugle blew.

Oh, how Pete hated to get up!

But Captain Cat

sprang right out of bed.

He had to check out the garbage

before it was taken away.

Then it was time for inspection.

Everybody lined up.

Captain Cat lined up, too.

The general fixed a soldier's gun.

He fixed Pete's hat.

All he could fix for Captain Cat were his whiskers.

"Forward march!" said the general.

The soldiers went one way.

Captain Cat went the other way.

He had to chase some birds.

The soldiers crawled

in the mud.

They hiked

through rain and sleet.

But not Captain Cat!

He was taking a nap

on Pete's bed.

Time for chow!

Pete and the other soldiers

rushed into the mess hall

to get plates of nice, hot food.

Captain Cat wished

Pete would get him

a plate with a mouse.

"Are you my buddy?" asked Pete.

"Me-ow," said Captain Cat.

Lights out!

Everyone went to sleep

and dreamed of loved ones.

Captain Cat dreamed

of his loved one, too.